You are Chaylo. On the way to your Star Ranger clubhouse, you see a strange scientist fiddling around with Space Fleet's new experimental spaceship. You decide to follow him and see what he's up to. Maybe this is your chance to catch a spy!

You might be a kid, but you're brave and smart — smart enough to stay out of trouble . . . you hope!

Chasing the spy through space, your ship is attacked by strange blobby creatures that make you lose speed!

Will you go outside the spaceship and try to remove the creatures before they damage it, maybe losing sight of the spy?

Or do you want to ignore the creatures, hoping to catch the spy before he escapes with the ship forever?

The choice is yours!

Star Rangers and the Spy

by Jean Blashfield
and
Beverly Charette

Illustrated by Mario Macari, Jr.
Cover art by Joe DeVelasco

TSR, Inc.
PRODUCTS OF YOUR IMAGINATION™

Stop!

Don't turn this page yet!

You're about to set out on not one, but many great adventures in the Frontier of space! Here's all you have to do—

To start your adventure, turn to page 7 and begin. Read until you come to a set of choices. Pick one and follow the directions.

As you read, keep making choices and following directions until the story ends. Then start at the beginning again and pick other choices. Each one will take you on a different adventure.

All right, go ahead and turn the page . . .

"HALT!"

Your feet stop so quickly that your top half keeps moving, and you fall flat. OOF!

Gasping for breath, you raise your head and look around to see who yelled at you.

A short distance away from you in a small guardhouse stands a Space Fleet guard. He controls the electronic opening in the fence around a special launch pad. And he's not looking at you!

Glad that you weren't doing anything wrong, you watch the eight-legged Vrusk guard hold out his hand toward a human in a scientist's long white coat.

Your father is a scientist for the United Planets here on your home planet of Nedram, so you know most of the scientists at Space Fleet Headquarters. But you don't recognize this man.

The scientist quickly sticks some file folders under his arm and shuffles through papers from his pocket. Then he holds one up before the guard.

The guard pushes a button inside the guardhouse, and the blue glow in the opening

disappears. "You can go in now, Mr. Drel," you hear the Vrusk say. "What time will you want to come out?"

TIME! You're late! You were running to your Star Rangers meeting when you fell. Scrambling to your feet, you brush blue dust off the front of your Rangers uniform.

As you turn on Perky, the Personal Radio Computer Kit on your wrist, to call the clubhouse, you hear the scientist say, "I won't be long. I just have to check the rocket panels of the *X-302*. Oh, by the way. I'll leave by the other exit."

The scientist goes through the opening and walks toward the *X-302*, the same experimental spaceship your father works on.

You see the file folder the man stuck under his arm fall to the ground behind him.

"Hey!" you shout. "You dropped some papers!" But the man doesn't hear you and hurries on, nearly stepping on a Boxil, one of Space Fleet's cube-shaped messengers.

You dash up to the guard, who is an old friend. "Kwist, that man dropped something!"

The Vrusk stands stiff and salutes you smartly, with a smile. "Ranger Chaylo, sir!"

Pleased that he notices your uniform, you return the salute.

"I can't leave my post, Chaylo," the guard says, "but why don't you run and take the papers to him?" He turns off the blue glowing alarm signal again and you hurry in.

Swooping up the file folder, you dash around the *X-302*. The spaceship gleams gold in the glare of spotlights, almost ready to be launched for the first time.

You round the ship . . . and stop abruptly. The man in the white coat is standing very still, listening carefully and looking all around. His eyes are so dark, they are almost black. And they seem to take in everything.

As he turns toward you, you duck back behind a rocket nozzle. Why—you don't know. But suddenly, you think it would be better if he doesn't know that you've seen him!

Very slowly, you raise your head again, and you see Mr. Drel go into the ground control room at the side of the launch pad.

"But he was going to check the rocket panels!" you think. You continue to watch as the scientist runs through a computer

program in a room that is off limits to almost everyone but your father.

"He's not supposed to be in there," you say to yourself. "I bet he's a spy!"

Do you want to go tell the guard what you think? If so, turn to page 30.

If you want to watch the man a little longer, turn to page 21.

Maybe you should tiptoe away, go out the gate, and hurry to your Star Rangers meeting. If so, turn to page 34.

"There isn't enough time to do anything but follow him in our ship," you tell the others. "Climb aboard and take your positions."

Your friends, even Nanny Robot, strap themselves in at their space-travel stations.

A few minutes later, you see the *X-302*'s rocket thrusters blast fire and vapor, and the ship lifts off.

"Hang on, everybody," you shout over the roar of the other ship's rocket engines.

With a sputter and a POP! *Star Ranger 1*'s engines start up, and you blast out into space after the spy.

"How will we stop him?" Gogol asks.

"I don't know yet," you reply. "What's our speed, Rama?"

"Two hundred kerns and rising."

"What direction are we heading, Nanny?"

"Three-point-five degrees left of the fourth quadrant," the robot beeps.

"Straight toward the sector held by our enemies, the Sathars," you say. "Drel must be working for those evil creatures."

The *X-302* speeds through space faster and faster with *Star Ranger 1* close behind. But

you know if you don't do something soon, your ship will start falling behind.

"Carell," you say, "let's contact him."

Carell flicks a switch and says, "This is *Star Ranger 1*. Come in *X-302*. Over."

You hear only static from the speaker. But then the static clears, and you hear a gruff voice snarl, "I can hear you little brats. What do you want?"

"That's him! That's Drel!" you cry. "Tell him to turn around and surrender!"

Carell repeats your message.

"Turn around? Surrender? Ha!" Drel's voice laughs. "You better turn around, kids,

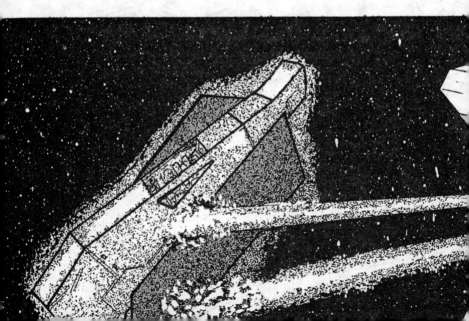

before it's too late! Over and out!"

"Chaylo! Look!" cries Gogol, pointing at the outside viewing screen.

Coming at you from out of a hatch in the side of the *X-302* are blobby creatures with many tentacles. As you watch, they hit your ship and stick there, slowing your speed.

Should you leave the ship and try to remove the creatures? Turn to page 72.

Or will you ignore them and keep chasing the spy? Turn to page 52.

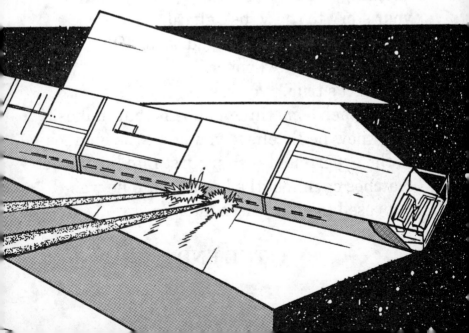

As you try to decide, Perky squawks again.
The Rangers must be trying to reach you. But
the harsh sound reminds you of why you are
here—you thought the man was a spy!

And that possibility hasn't changed just
because he showed you a neat video game.

Your thoughts must show on your face,
because the scientist's face suddenly looks less
friendly, and he starts toward you.

Leaping up, you dash out the hatch door,
across the ramp, and into the elevator.

Behind you, you hear, "Come back here!"

At ground level, you run toward the gate,
shouting, "Kwist! Kwist!" Quickly, you tell
your story to the Vrusk guard.

He looks at you sadly and says, "Oh,
Chaylo. What a whopper!"

"But it's true!" you cry.

Just then something happens that makes
you know he'll believe you now—the engines
of the experimental ship burst into life. Kwist
watches open-mouthed as the ship he was
supposed to guard rises into the sky.

THE END

Firing up *Star Ranger 1*'s thrusters, you follow Drel as he walks toward a storage shed near the back gate of the launch area.

Watching him on the viewing screen, you see him reach for a jetpack hanging on the side of the building and then turn as he notices your ship coming toward him.

"We've trapped you now," you say.

As if he can hear you, the spy turns and starts to run toward the exit, dropping the jetpack in his haste.

"Quick, Rama," you shout excitedly. "Block that exit! We just might catch a spy!"

The ship zooms over the spy, and Rama turns the thrusters down to shoot vapor between Drel and the gate just in time to stop him. Stumbling over a crate, he turns around and dashes for the main gate.

"That's just where we want him to go!" cries Gogol.

"I'd say we have enough proof to convince Kwist the guard to capture Mr. Drel," you say.

As you speak, Drel rounds the corner of a building and slams SMACK! into Kwist, and the two go sprawling in a pile of tangled arms and legs.

"Hooray!" you all shout as you land the ship and run down the ramp.

"Who? What . . . what's going on?" asks Kwist, dazed by the collision.

"Why, Kwist, you've just stopped this spy from escaping," you tell the confused guard, helping him to his feet. "He was going to steal the *X-302.*"

Rama and Gogol each take one of Drel's arms as he stands and hold him prisoner.

"If it weren't for you kids, I would have made it," growls Drel.

"Then good for you, Star Rangers," cheers Kwist. "Space Fleet owes you a big thank you."

You smile proudly and say, "For a Star Ranger, it's all in a day's work."

THE END

Silently, you peer around the rocket nozzle. The man in the ground control room keeps glancing at a paper in one hand and typing computer commands with the other.

Your father has shown you all around the *X-302.* You remember that the orange light you see glowing on the computer means that the navigation program is being run.

The man presses one last button and gathers his file folders. He smiles to himself as he walks toward the door. You duck out of sight as he walks by.

Moving as quietly as you can, you follow him around the experimental ship. You expect him to head for the far gate as he said he would. But instead he goes toward the elevator to the *X-302!*

SKWAK! A harsh sound sends you ducking frantically behind a transport crate.

The noise was Perky on your wrist. The other Star Rangers must be looking for you. "I hope he didn't hear it," you whisper to yourself. Your heart pounds in your chest.

Very, very carefully, you peer around the crate . . . but no one is in sight!

Where did he go? You look toward the elevator, but the light that goes on when it is in use isn't glowing. You run quietly back to the control room but see no one.

"Where is he?" you wonder, suddenly feeling scared. "Maybe I better go . . ."

"I've got you!" growls a voice as you feel a strong hand grab the hair on your head. Looking up, you see the white sleeve of the scientist's coat.

"Why are you following me, kid?"

"Following you? Me?" you squeak, trying to sound innocent. "I was just . . . just going to my Star Rangers meeting. The guard lets me cut through here."

You must have sounded truthful, because the hand gripping your hair relaxes a bit. You've got to decide quickly what to do!

If you try to escape, turn to page 64.

But if you stay with the scientist to learn if he's doing something wrong, turn to page 38.

"We can't waste any more time," you decide. "Let's follow this guy and see what he's up to. But we'll have to be careful."

"Now you're talking," agrees Rama. "We can fly our hover car to the launch pad."

As everyone piles into the small car, parked just below the clubhouse, you hurry to link Perky with the clubhouse computer just in case you need them both.

The ship blasts off and you arrive at the launch pad in a matter of seconds.

"Back so soon, Ranger Chaylo?" the Vrusk guard asks, surprised.

Mumbling something about a Ranger field

trip, you and your hover car are allowed to pass through the gates.

Near the launch pad you park next to *Star Ranger 1*. Placing Nanny on board the spaceship, the four of you spread out and slip into hiding places close to the experimental ship's ground control room.

At a large computer terminal, Mr. Drel, the scientist, is typing the commands for a program. Every few seconds he looks around to see if anyone is watching. Finally, he pushes the buttons that begin to release the mechanical arms holding the ship in place.

You've seen enough and silently signal the

other Rangers to regroup near *Star Ranger 1*. Everyone creeps silently back to the ship.

"It looks to me as if he's reprogrammed the primary computer to take off," you say. "He's going to steal the *X-302!*"

"Let's follow him and blast him out of the sky!" exclaims Rama dramatically.

"That might be difficult to do since this ship isn't equipped with weapons," says Carell, knowing Rama doesn't mean it.

"We could try to fix the ship so that it can't take off," you offer.

"Or you could tell Admiral Shuk at Space Fleet Command," beeps Nanny Robot.

"We have proof now," adds Gogol.

Will you tell someone at Space Fleet Command? Turn to page 66.

If you think you can stop the ship from taking off, turn to page 53.

If you want to follow the experimental ship in Star Ranger 1 and hope somehow to stop the spy, turn to page 12.

The door to the bridge flies open, and suddenly you know you don't have the courage to let yourself be caught.

You scoot out of the chair and back through the sliding door. It thunks into place just as the spy enters the bridge.

With your ear to the door, you can just hear Drel say, "What's this? I must have hit the wrong button as I stood up. Well, I'll fix all the numbers."

Your heart sinks, and you slump against the door as you feel the ship change course.

You know it's entering the Void. But you have no idea where you'll come out!

Hours later, you feel the ship landing. The sliding door opens and Drel leans in, an evil smile on his face.

"Come on, kid. You were so busy being nosy that you nosy-ed yourself right onto a planet where the Sathar keep prisoners."

As he shoves you out the hatch door, you look out on an alien planet and know you'll probably never get home.

THE END

Maybe this is your chance to catch a spy!

But then you remember Kwist, who guards the gate. It's his job to catch spies.

Taking a last look at the mysterious man, you tiptoe back toward the gate.

"Kwist!" you call in a loud whisper.

"Is that you, Chaylo?" The Vrusk guard pokes his head out of the guardhouse.

"Do you know that guy who went in?"

"Sure. He's a scientist named Drel."

"Have you ever seen him before?"

"No—but he's got all the right forms admitting him to the launch pad."

"He said he was going to check the rocket panels. But he didn't. He looked around to see if anyone was watching, and then I saw him do something to the computer in the ground control room. I think he's a spy."

"Ah, Chaylo. You must think you're a policeman." And the guard turns away.

"But, Kwist . . ." you start to say.

"I can't play games now," he says.

Please go back to page 11 and make another choice.

You watch on the viewing screen as the spy takes a jetpack hanging from the side of a storage shed and blasts off, away from the launch area.

"Should we tell someone at Space Fleet Command about what we saw?" Gogol asks.

You sigh. "Nobody would believe a group of kids. Besides, he knows someone is on to him. I don't think he'll be back."

"Then there's nothing left to do but go home," says Carell.

You fire up *Star Ranger 1* and head back to the clubhouse.

A few weeks later, you're watching your favorite television show when a news bulletin flashes across the screen.

"We interrupt this program," says the announcer, "to bring you the latest news on the attack of the Sathars on the planet Loftu."

You move closer to the screen as the picture changes from the announcer's face to the scene of a space battle.

"Earlier today," the newsman continues, "Loftu was attacked by Sathar fighter ships accompanied by a new, deadly spaceship no one has ever seen before. Rumor has it that the craft is an experimental ship stolen from Space Fleet headquarters."

You gasp in horror as the *X-302* appears on the television screen firing laser missiles at the planet.

"Oh, no!" you cry. "The spy must have worked for our enemies, the Sathars, and they equipped the ship with weapons."

You stare helplessly at the screen and watch the planet's destruction by the ship you could have stopped.

THE END

As you run, you look up and then stop abruptly as you spot a red weather lab high above you in midair. You smile, remembering how you talked your father into giving the Rangers the abandoned lab for a clubhouse.

Gasping for breath, you fumble for the "propel" button to your jetpack, find it, press it, and WHOOSH! you are jet-powered to the door. Once there, you press your palm against a blue square sensor, the door slides open, and you dash through.

"Well, it's about time you got here," scolds Rama, your friend, a Yazirian. A frown darkens her monkeylike face.

"I'm sorry, but I have a good reason for being late," you say, and you rush to tell everyone about the man at the launch pad.

"He sounds dangerous," says Gogol, a Dralasite Ranger, after you finish. His rubbery skin wrinkles with worry.

"I must admit the human's actions do seem peculiar," Carell the eight-legged Vrusk comments.

"Peculiar? He sounds like a spy to me!" cries Rama. "Let's go capture him."

"But we need proof," you point out.

"Let's follow him," Carell suggests.

"Any Star Ranger leaving this sector of Interplanetary Space," a high-pitched electronic voice pipes up, "must be accompanied by a registered robot router."

You groan as Nanny Navigator Robot rolls up to interrupt the discussion. Her red, yellow, and blue lights flash her concern.

Assigned to your unit of Star Rangers, she directs your course and travels with you every time you fly your ship, *Star Ranger 1*.

"Maybe we should tell someone in authority," says Gogol, ignoring the robot. "If this guy really is a spy, he certainly won't like us following him."

"Oh, phooey!" snaps Rama. "We can handle him."

Will you follow the suspicious scientist with your friends? Turn to page 24.

Or will you tell someone at Space Fleet headquarters about him? Turn to page 66.

You move your head slightly under the scientist's hand and know that you could probably wriggle free. But you also know that the *X-302*—Space Fleet's special ship!—might be in danger. If you stay, you might be able to stop it.

"Since you're so interested in what I'm doing, why don't you come on up and see?" says the scientist. He pulls you toward the elevator to the ramp of the *X-302*.

You ride the elevator with Mr. Drel, and for a moment you feel panic, wondering if it's too late to try to get away.

When the doors open, he leads you across the ramp to the main hatch of the ship.

Inside the ship, the scientist looks thoughtful for a moment and then says, "I've got something you'll be interested in."

You breathe a sigh of relief when the scientist leaves you standing by the hatch and walks over to a large instrument panel covered with switches, buttons, dials, and small television screens.

As you watch, the scientist flicks a switch and a computer screen comes to life. He presses a yellow button and the words

"COSMIC CRUSADER" appear in color.

"Come over and try this game. Just talk into the microphone and tell the computer what you want the Cosmic Crusader to do."

"But . . . " You stop. Video games on an experimental ship! It doesn't make sense! You stand there, afraid to come toward the scientist, even though he seems friendly.

"Well, then, turn on your Perky," Mr. Drel says, laughing.

You are puzzled, but you do as he says and turn on your wrist computer. The game appears on Perky's small screen!

The game looks as if it might be fun, but it's hard to see it on the small screen. Looking up at the big screen on the console, you move over to it and start playing.

TWANG! The Cosmic Crusader shoots laser arrows at the fire-breathing Dromo monsters. Then the action stops until you press the controls and shout, "Laser arrows away!"

You play the game for a few minutes until you notice that Drel is doing something to the flight instruments. You had forgotten about the ship!

You look at the open hatch behind you.

Your eyes turn to the video game, which is frozen, waiting for your command.

You think about the scientist's pleasant laugh and kindly voice.

But you also remember the suspicious things he did in the ground control room.

Do you want to run for the open hatch? If so, turn to page 16.

Do you want to stay on board to see if you can learn the truth? Turn to page 47.

You discover it's hard for you to operate your wrist computer while you're wearing the bulky spacesuit, but you manage.

In a few seconds, you have found the correct program on the clubhouse computer. As you concentrate hard, you type in on Perky the commands to change *Star Ranger 1*'s outer structure to a slippery material.

"That should do it," you say when you're done. You look up from your wrist. "Whoops!" you say, floating backwards into space. You had been concentrating so hard on the program, you forgot you were on top of the ship!

"Now, let's all float a short distance away from the ship and see what happens," you tell Rama and Nanny Robot.

As the three of you float back, you notice a slight movement in one of the creatures. It starts to tremble, and then suddenly, one of its tentacles pops free of the ship! Then another tentacle pops loose. And another.

"The program's working!" Rama shouts. "The outer surface is changing."

In a few minutes, tentacles on all the

creatures are popping free. Soon all the spore creatures have lost their hold on your ship and are headed back toward the *X-302*.

You, Rama, and Nanny head back inside the ship through the airlock. As you remove your helmet, you hear static coming from the speaker and then Mr. Drel's voice, sounding much higher than before.

"This is *X-302* to *Star Ranger 1*. Help! I can't get these slimy things off the ship. Can you get them off for me?"

Everyone bursts out laughing at the voice of the frightened spy. You finally manage to say, "*Star Ranger 1* to *X-302*. We read you and can help you under one condition—that you surrender to us."

The speaker is silent for a moment, and then you hear, "All right. Take the ship. Do whatever you want. Just get me away from these creatures!"

"You heard what the man said," you say. "Let's capture the ship and bring it home!"

THE END

"Who's going to believe me when I'm not sure he's doing something wrong?" you think.

You keep playing the video game, but your mind is really on what Drel is doing.

Out of the corner of your eye, you watch the scientist begin to talk to a strange figure that appears on a television screen.

"... on board ... deliver ... *302* tomorrow," he whispers. You lean closer, trying to hear.

"You little spy!" he shouts, jumping up.

He caught you listening to him!

ZIP! You dash through a doorway. ZAP! You hit the blue sensor on the door and it slides shut. You lean against it, panting.

"You're the spy!" you shout through the door. You can see Drel's angry, red face through a window on the door.

"But you'll never tell anyone!" Drel yells back. Suddenly, you realize that the floor beneath you is trembling.

"Hang on, kid!" Drel shouts gleefully. THE SHIP IS TAKING OFF!

Before you can do it yourself, the force caused by the ship speeding up sits you down! Frightened by this unexpected trip into space, you wonder how you will stop Drel now. Then you hear Mr. Drel's voice.

Listening carefully, you hear Drel receive instrument settings over the radio. He's going to change the ship's destination!

You hit the sensor and the door slides open. Drel, his back to you, is too busy to notice. You crawl forward and listen.

"I'll change the navigation settings as you told me. They'll take the ship through the Void." He gives an evil laugh. "And Space Fleet won't know until it's too late that the Sathar have stolen their ship!"

Sathar! The Sathar are the enemy of the United Planets! And once the ship enters the Void—that strange place where spaceships can travel faster than the speed of light—he can take it anywhere!

Whispering into Perky, you radio an SOS to Space Fleet Patrol. But you don't know if it has been heard. And if it was heard, you don't know how long it will take for help to reach you. What else can you do?

You can try to keep Drel from making the changes. Turn to page 60.

Or you can try to fix what he messes up. Turn to page 70.

You decide to ignore the creatures. You tell Rama, "Increase speed." *Star Ranger 1* zooms faster after the *X-302*. Soon you are gaining on the larger ship.

"Maybe we can get close enough to link the two ships," you say excitedly.

But just as *Star Ranger 1* is about to touch the *X-302*, you hear the engines in your little ship start to cough and sputter.

"The creatures are blocking the rocket thrust nozzles," beeps Nanny Robot.

"We'll have to turn around," Rama cries.

As you turn the ship around and head for home, you feel terrible.

"We failed," you say quietly. "And it's my fault for ignoring those creatures."

Nanny hands you a tissue from the drawer in her middle section. "That's all right, Chaylo. At least you tried to stop Drel."

Blowing your nose into the tissue, you nod your head. "I guess you're right, Nanny. But who knows what evil things Mr. Drel will do with that special ship?"

THE END

"My father's told me a lot about the *X-302*," you say. "I think I know a way we can keep the ship from blasting off. But we'll have to be quiet and very careful."

"Then let's get going," says Rama.

The four of you sneak down your ship's ramp and hide behind an orange transport crate. The spy is nowhere in sight. Then you see him through a window in the *X-302*.

"We'll have to hurry. He's already on board," you whisper. "Here's the plan. We'll all ride the elevator to the ship's platform. Then Rama will go to the rear of the ship and disconnect the back-up engine."

"How do I do that?" asks Rama.

"Just leave the door to the compartment open," you say. "That should do it."

You turn to Carell and say, "You guard the main hatch. Give us a signal if you see the spy coming out."

"What about me?" Gogol asks you.

"You're coming with me. Grab that screwdriver and we'll use it to pry open the the engine panel in the side of the ship."

Your heart pounds as you all ride the elevator. When the doors open, Carell and Rama creep to their positions. Then you and Gogol crouch low and run to yours.

Beside the *X-302*, you carefully pry off the panel so the spy will not hear you. With your fingers, you unwind a red wire from around a bolt. Then you do the same with a green wire, a blue wire, and a purple and white striped wire.

"Are you sure you know what you're doing?" Gogol whispers.

"I think so," you whisper back. "Dad said these wires connect the last electronic sequence for ignition."

When you finish unwinding the wires, you quietly close the panel, signal to Carell and Rama, and creep back to *Star Ranger 1.*

"I sure hope this works," says Rama.

"It looks as if it will," says Carell.

On the outside viewing screen, you can see the *X-302* begin to lift off. Your heart sinks. But instead of clouds of vapor from engine thrusters, you see a little puff of smoke—poof! The *X-302* hovers in the air for a moment and lands CRASH! on the launch pad. You all cheer!

Then, as you watch, you see Drel stomp out onto the ship's platform. His face is beet-red, and his eyes are wild.

"He's not very happy." Gogol chuckles.

Drel hurries to the main engine panel, opens it, and looks inside. Closing it suddenly, he looks around as if he expects to see someone and steps into the elevator. Lucky for you, he doesn't notice your spaceship, which is hidden by fuel tanks and storage buildings.

"Look," says Carell. "He's leaving."

When the elevator doors open at the bottom, Drel starts to walk rapidly away from the *X-302* toward the launch pad gate.

"We can't just let him go!" cries Rama.

"But he looks awfully angry," says Gogol, "and dangerous."

You consider your choices and then say,

"He's too dangerous to follow. Besides, we spoiled his plan. What more can he do?" Turn to page 31.

"We can chase him in STAR RANGER 1 and block his exit." Turn to page 17.

Together, you, Rama, and Nanny pull on the tentacle of one of the creatures. Out of the corner of your eye, you see the *X-302* fire its thrusters and take off.

Finally, you break the tentacle's grip with a loud POP! Hooray! The creature drifts away. You keep removing tentacles until each creature has drifted off into space.

Back inside the ship, you let air back into the air lock and remove your helmet. At once you notice the air seems different.

"It feels cold in here, and the air smells funny," you say to the others.

"Oh, no!" cries Gogol. "Those spores must have broken our protective shield."

You turn to Carell. "Quickly, we must head home before our air supply leaks out."

Carell turns the ship around.

You drop into your seat, feeling terrible. "We let Drel get away," you say.

Nanny Robot reaches across from her seat and places a hand of nuts and bolts on your shoulder. "But at least you tried, Chaylo."

THE END

You suddenly know that you CAN'T let the ship go off course into the unknown! You think about what you can do.

You could knock the spy out. You could turn off the ship's false gravity and, when Drel is weightless, set him spinning. You could lasso him with . . .

Well, you guess none of those things would really work. But you COULD unplug the navigation computer!

Peering over a high-backed seat, you study the cords running along the floor to the computers. You trace a thick red one going

from the fuel cells to the navigation computer.

Certain that at any minute Drel will realize you're on the bridge, you crawl toward where the red cord joins another cord going to the fuel cells. Hand, knee, hand, knee . . . you concentrate on crawling silently. Drel is still working at the computer.

Then you grab the two cords and yank with all your might until they pull apart.

The screen goes dead! Drel turns in his seat and sees you. His face is red with anger.

"You brat! You've ruined it all!"

The spy pounds furiously on the work table

in front of him, and you know he wishes it were you! Suddenly, he rises, and he seems bigger and fiercer than before.

You grab at the switch on your backpack, and just as Drel reaches for you, the jetpack zooms to life and lifts you away from his clutching fingers.

"ARGGGGHHHH!" he shrieks, and he reaches for you again. Quickly, you twist your body, so the jetpack zooms you away from his grasp again.

The bridge of the *X-302* is small, so you have to twist and turn, rise and fall, to keep him from grabbing you. You don't know how long you can keep it up.

"I'll get you!" he shouts, and you're afraid he might . . . until you zoom past a window and see, coming up fast, the small, swift rescue ships of Space Fleet Patrol.

You raise Perky and shout happily into it, "Space Fleet Patrol, this is Ranger Chaylo, in control!"

THE END

You don't know for sure whether or not the scientist is really doing something wrong. But you decide that you don't want to find out all by yourself!

Moving your head a bit, you discover that the large hand on your head isn't twisted quite so firmly in your hair. Maybe you can run away without ending up bald.

You relax slightly and then twist suddenly out of the man's grasp. You're free! As you run quickly toward the main gate, your head feels tingly all over.

"Hey, kid!" the scientist calls after you. "Where are you off to in such a hurry?" And he laughs.

As you pass the guardhouse, you wonder if you should tell Kwist what has happened. But you realize there's nothing to tell. After all, the man laughed when you ran. Maybe he's not doing anything wrong at all.

Running at top speed now, you hurry to your Star Ranger clubhouse.

Please turn to page 34.

"Is this your idea of a prank, Chaylo?" booms Admiral Shuk. "Why, I understand Mr. Drel is one of our finest scientists. At least, I think it was Mr. Drel."

Standing at attention in front of the admiral's desk, you feel your face go red. "But, sir, don't you agree that his actions seem, well . . . suspicious?"

"I'm sure Mr. Drel has some reason for behaving that way," says the admiral. "Now, why don't you and your friends leave the capture of spies to us here at Space Fleet?"

"Yes, sir." You salute.

Returning your salute, Admiral Shuk adds, "We'll keep this incident between you and me, Ranger Chaylo. Your father doesn't need to know about it." He winks at you and returns to the papers on his desk.

You turn and march out of the admiral's office followed by your fellow Star Rangers.

The moment the door closes behind you, Rama cries, "He doesn't believe anything you told him! He thinks it's all a joke!"

Standing in the hallway in front of the admiral's office, the four of you are jostled by passing officers, scientists, and workers, all wearing the Space Fleet emblem.

"Shhhhhh!" scolds Gogol. "Not so loud."

"I wouldn't worry that we're bothering anyone," says Carell. "Like the admiral, everyone at Space Fleet is ignoring us."

"Well, at least we tried," says Gogol.

"But we can't just give up," says Rama.

Carell shakes his head. "You heard the admiral. We're supposed to leave this matter to Space Fleet."

You all hang your heads in defeat.

Then a thought hits you and you say quietly, "We're Space Fleet. Star Rangers is a unit of Space Fleet."

"We'll get into a lot of trouble with Admiral Shuk if he finds out we're following Mr. Drel," warns Carell.

"Yes, if ALL of us go," you agree. "But not if only one goes. I'll sneak aboard the *X-302* by myself," you explain.

"But you can't go alone, it's too dangerous," cries Gogol.

"Don't worry, Gogol." You pat your friend's shoulder. "I've got Perky in case I need to contact you in the clubhouse."

Before anyone else can disagree, you say good-bye and run off down the hallway and out of the building.

In a matter of minutes, you're back at the X-302's launch pad. Hidden behind an orange transport crate, you look all around and see no sign of the scientist.

Thinking he must be on board the X-302, you creep over to the elevator leading to the main hatch of the ship. Trembling with excitement, you ride to the top of the lift. When the doors open, you cross the ramp and peek inside the open door of the hatch.

"That's strange," you think. "The entrance is never left open." You slowly step forward into the ship.

Suddenly, a hand grabs you from behind, and you whirl around to face Mr. Drel!

"Aha! I've caught you, you little spy!" he growls.

Before you can think, you twist free and run through an open door, which slides closed behind you. You lean against it, panting.

Please turn to page 48.

As you peek out at the spy, he seems to look larger and more evil than he did before. The computer is very complicated, but it looks easier to handle than Mr. Drel!

You wait impatiently until he punches one final button and says, "That's it!" He rises and leaves the bridge.

Creeping silently across the room, you go to the console, thinking that you can probably reload the original navigation program.

You type in "CATALOG" and a list of programs appears on the screen. The only one that looks likely is "FLITETESTNAV/4a."

You type "LOAD FLITETESTNAV/4a" and cross your fingers. The computer whirs for a moment. Then it asks, "ABORT NEWNAV?"

You're just answering "YES" when you hear Drel returning.

If you quickly run away from Drel and hide before the program is loaded, turn to page 28.

But if you stay there and finish running the program, turn to page 75.

"Those creatures are slowing us down," you say. "Come on, Rama. Let's go outside and somehow get them off."

You open a compartment that holds your life-support spacesuits and jetpacks. You and the Yazirian step into your suits.

Just as you're about to pull the helmet over your head, you hear your robot guardian quote from the Nanny Navigator Manual: " 'No Ranger may leave the vehicle while in space without a qualified Nanny Robot.' "

You shrug. "Okay, Nanny. Let's go."

The three of you step into the air lock chamber. Unlike you and Rama, Nanny

doesn't need a spacesuit. The "air" she
breathes is electronic energy, not oxygen.

When all the air in the compartment has
been sucked out to match the vacuum of
space, you unlock and open the outside door,
take one step, and float out into space.

For a moment, you enjoy the feeling of
being weightless. Then you use your jetpack
to send you to the top of your ship. From there
you can see that the X-302 has stopped.

Nanny, connected by a cord to the ship's
computer, and Rama join you.

Up close, you see that the creatures are

plastered onto your ship like gum. You try to pry off one of the tentacles and the effort pushes you backward into space. Your jetpack shoots you back to the ship. Rama tries to pry one off with the same result.

"These creatures are stuck tight," you report to Carell and Gogol inside the ship.

"According to the computer, they're galactic spores," Carell replies. "Theycan change their surface structure to match anything at which they are fired."

"So," you hear Gogol say, "each creature has become a part of the ship."

Nanny beeps, "The outer structure of the ship could be changed to a slippery substance to free it from the spores, Chaylo."

"I just learned that program," you say. "But I'm not sure I can do it right."

You think for a moment then say,

"I'll use Perky to recall the program from the clubhouse computer." Turn to page 43.

"I'd probably mess up the program. Let's pry them off, Rama." Turn to page 59.

You hold your breath, watching the words on the screen. "NAVIGATION PROGRAM LOADING" seems to stay there forever!

The door to the bridge opens.

"Rotten kid!" the spy shouts as he sees you on the bridge. Your heart is in your throat as he starts to come toward you.

Then the words appear, "PROGRAM LOADED."

"What are you doing?" shrieks Drel.

Just as his hand reaches toward you, you type "RUN PROGRAM." He tries to jerk you out of the seat, but you buckle your seat belt and press the button labeled "PITCH."

Suddenly, the whole ship tilts. Your seat belt holds you, but Drel is sent sprawling against the wall.

Then you hear the voice of the computer say, "Now entering the Void."

Since it's too late for Drel to change the ship's direction, you hit the button labeled "LEVEL," and the ship's balance is restored. Drel scrambles to his feet.

Now you both can do nothing but wait while you pass through the Void. A few minutes later, the computer says, "The Void has been cleared. Destination ahead."

Hoping you loaded the program in time, you rush to a window. Drel is there, too.

Ahead of you is a planet you've never seen before. But coming toward you is a wonderful sight—Space Fleet Patrol ships! You landed in friendly territory!

Drel slumps to the floor, moaning, "All our plans are ruined because of a kid!"

You return to the console and say into the microphone, "Ranger Chaylo, in control!"

THE END

ENDLESS QUEST™ Books
From the producers of the
DUNGEON & DRAGON® Game

For a free catalog, write
TSR, Inc.
P.O. Box 756, Dept. EQB
Lake Geneva, WI 53147

TSR, Inc.
PRODUCTS OF YOUR IMAGINATION™

DUNGEON!
ADVENTURE GAME

A FANTASY BOARDGAME FOR THE ENTIRE FAMILY!

The same thrill of discovery you found in the FANTASY FOREST™ books can be enjoyed by the entire family in the DUNGEON® fantasy boardgame.

Become an elf, hero, superhero, or even a wizard in search of great treasure in a deep dungeon.

It's fast,, fun, and full of surprises — the DUNGEON! game from the game wizards at TSR.

For a free catalog write:

TSR, Inc. TSR (UK), Ltd.
POB 756 The Mill, Rathmore Road
Lake Geneva, Cambridge CB14AD
WI 53147 United Kingdom

FANTASY FOREST™ Books

Is your dragon dragging?

Do you both need to go on an adventure?

Why not Pick a Path to Adventure™ with these
FANTASY FOREST™ Books?

#1 THE RING, THE SWORD, AND THE UNICORN
#2 RUINS OF RANGAR
#3 SHADOWCASTLE
#4 KEEP OF THE ANCIENT
#5 DUNGEON OF DARKNESS
#6 STAR RANGERS AND THE SPY

From the producers of the DUNGEONS & DRAGONS® Game

For a free catalog, write:

TSR, Inc.
P. O. Box 756, Dept. FF
Lake Geneva, WI 53147